The Gambit Gang

Walking In Between The Waterways

The Gambit Gang

The Gambit Gang

Walking In Between the Waterways

Johanna Chojnicki

Illustrated by Estelle Chojnicki

The Gambit Gang

First Edition

Printed in the United States of America

Edited by:
Judith Hilovsky and Estelle Chojnicki

The Gambit Gang

Walking In Between the Waterways

Chapters

The Gambit Gang

As I walk in the water, I feel something
change.
As I walk in the water, I see a new
landscape.
A landscape that has big tall trees with little
ones in between.

As I walk in the water, I smell a new smell,
Cold, crisp air, sweetness, and a storm.

As I walk in the water,
I turn to see if I can go back from whence, I
came.

Now, whenever I am in the water,
I go to the other side.

I am not alone.
there are others like me.

We are the Gambit Gang,
For we walk in between the waterways!

The Gambit Gang

Prologue

A little girl came running down the wooded path ahead of her family towards the waterfall behind their house. She has long dark brown hair, hazel eyes, and pale skin. Her name is Johanna. Johanna loves to go down to her Papa's waterfalls to play in the water and find fossils. Today she reached the falls long before her family. She took off her socks, shoes and walked into the cool clear water. She walked up the stream a little farther than usual today and noticed something was different. She looked around and noticed the trees were taller, the river wider, and instead of smelling hot, humid air, it felt cold and crisp, with a sweetness of a storm. She looked around again and was startled to see a wolf staring at her. The wolf started to walk towards her, and while it was walking, it was transforming into a humanoid form with a wolf-like face. It had a tail and fur all over but was walking upright like a human. When it came closer, she noticed he had on jeans, a plaid shirt, and a denim jacket. The wolf wore spectacles and had a beautiful walking cane.

As the wolf approached, he said, "You must be Johanna, Joan's granddaughter. I am a friend of hers. My name is Dr. Wolf."

A little scared but curious, Johanna said, "I know someone named Dr. Wolf."

Dr. Wolf laughed and said, "I know who you are talking about, he is a good man. How is your Grandmother? I haven't seen her in a long time."

"Grandma Joan died when I was a baby, and my Aunt Jo died just a few days ago."

Dr. Wolf frowned and said, "That's sad to hear. Until we meet again, Johanna." And just like that he transformed back into a full wolf and ran back into the woods and disappeared.

The Gambit Gang

CHAPTER 1

The Adventure Begins

CRASH! CRACK! CRASH! CRACK!

"It's coming fast!

Mira isn't back yet!

And that giant troll is gaining on us!!"

"How are we going to capture this thing,

15Jo!?!" yelled Tommy short of

breath as we ran for our lives.

"Tommy keep up! We need to outrun this thing

until Mira gets the other one sent to headquarters!" I

yelled. "I can't keep this up much longer! Where is

she?!!" whined Tommy.

Zoom, zoom, zoom.

Mira yelled, "Sorry, I'm late! Took me longer than I thought to get that darn troll! What's the plan?"

"Mira, you will cut the troll off and create a vortex. Tommy, you and I will set a net of digital devices on all four sides of it so when the troll falls into the net it will be digitized and sent off to headquarters. Alright?"

Mira reacted at once using her superpower speed to cut off the troll. Tommy and I set out our net of devices. I set the south and west devices, and Tommy placed the north and east ones. A couple of minutes later we heard a loud thud. Mira ran so fast she created a vortex that sucked up all the air, making the troll pass out falling perfectly into our digitized net sending the troll into a computerized world at headquarters. Perfect!!

"Did you capture the other troll?" I asked Mira.

She nodded and passed out under the tree from pure exhaustion. I looked to my right and saw

Tommy was out cold too. I was glad to have them on my team.

Mira and Tommy were both smaller than me. Mira has dark brown eyes, black hair, and olive skin, and is super hyper. Sometimes she would talk so fast the words would all slur together and you would have no clue what the heck she was saying. Tommy, on the other hand was our whiny tech guy. He has olive skin, bed head dark blond hair, and hazel brown eyes. At least he's dependable and does his work.

Letting them get a few more minutes of rest, I collected our devices.

"Come on guys, wake up. I know you're tired, but we need to get back to base."

We started the long walk back through the woods to the portal. The spring was glowing through the trees; the portal was open. We walked into the spring and resurfaced on the other side back at base. Headquarters was a giant tree filled with rooms. The branches were used for training grounds. There was more housing in some of the smaller trees around it too.

"Go get your rest. I'll finish up and report in," I said.

They nodded and said good night. I took the elevator to the top floor where the head counselor stayed. All teams must report to their counselor after missions. Our counselor was Dr. Jambar Wolf. His office was decorated with rock and roll memorabilia from the 60s through 90s. He had photos on his desk. I recognized most of them, two I didn't. On one side of the office was a little nook for napping.

It was late and everybody must have gone home. That is, except Sandy. His real name is George O'Gale, but I called him Sandy because he can make sand that can put you to sleep or paralyze you. I heard Sandy had been a Secret Keeper from the day he could walk, but I had never seen him assigned to any missions nor to a team. Sandy is a year older than me, and he has never liked me. He is tall with spiky red hair, moon-like eyes, and pale skin. It was he and Dr. Wolf who trained me. He was wearing a white collared shirt, blue jeans, and sneakers. Leaning against a propped open door with his legs crossed. He looked extremely grumpy.

"What's the matter with you?" I asked.

"Good, you're back," said Dr. Wolf. "Come on in I have something to tell you. Have a seat."

I did, but Sandy didn't.

"So, what's up?" I asked.

Dr. Wolf replied, "George is going to stay with you at your house and lead your team."

I was shocked. "What?!? Why!? Sandy hasn't been on a mission before!"

Dr. Wolf looked at me with disappointment, "His name is George, not Sandy. He has gone on missions and led many of them. However, it has been quite some time, so I'm putting him in charge of your team to help him get his feet wet again. Then see if he is ready to handle assignments on his own."

"Then why are you putting him in charge of my team? Why can't he lead someone else's team? You know how much we fight.," I said angrily.

Sandy spoke smoothly, "There are reasons for which you do not need to know, and this is an order coming from your head counselor who happens to oversee the base, so you should just do what he says! *Miss. Rapunzel*!"

"*I am not blonde, you know!!* And you can't call me Rapunzel since I'm a brunette."

Dumb-dumb Sandy had decided to give me that nickname to tick me off since I have super long brown hair that never stops growing.

"Silence, both of you!" Dr. Wolf said while he banged his cane. We froze. He continued, "Now this discussion is over. Go home, go to bed, and expect a mission soon. I'll let Tommy and Mira know about the changes. Good night."

In the elevator, I asked Sandy, "What do you know about the rumors about Dr. Wolf?"   "What brought this on suddenly?"

"I was thinking about Dr. Wolf's magic. How he uses his cane."

When the elevator doors opened, Sandy said, "It is not my place to tell others' secrets."

CHAPTER 2

Schools In

Sandy and I stepped through the elevator doors into the courtyard of my house in Ladera Ranch, California. The elevator was a portal that could connect any two places. Headquarters has set them up to make it easy for the teams to get around quickly.

"I'm not going to bed, you go ahead," Sandy said.

"We have school tomorrow so don't stay up," I replied.

I went into my casita locking the glass door behind me and crawled into bed. I immediately dozed off into a dream. My dreams were usually strange, but this one was the weirdest. I saw a white building in a desert on top of a cliff overlooking a beach that looked like a prison. I saw a path that led to it. Within my first step I was already in front of the prison. I took another step and I was inside a cell with beautiful, strange butterflies. Somehow, I realized this wasn't a dream. It was a real place. I knew it and I was alone. The butterflies, glowing in different colors, were flying all around me. One had a broken wing, I reached out but when I touched it, the butterfly turned to blue dust.

The scene changed. I was now in a laboratory. There was a technician who looked ready to inject something into a fairy. I jumped towards them and with my left hand reached out to touch the fairy.

"What are you doing? Get away from that thing."

The scene changed again to a massive graveyard where I saw two old men. The first was very tall, almost eight feet, bald, and skinny. His skin was green and textured like a snake's. He was wearing a lab coat, black pants, and brown shoes. The second man was shorter, extremely muscular, with short blond hair, and skin covered in weird markings that looked like some language. The marked man spoke with a young voice, and I realized he wasn't old at all.

"Look at all these kills, and some are mine," he said standing amongst the graves. "Have you made any improvements to the serum?"

The snake man answered with a hissing voice while checking his phone. "The serum is almost ready for testing. I just got an alarm on my phone that a girl is in my laboratory." He looks quizzically at his accomplice. "What do you think of this?"

"Turn around and take a good look at her," the marked boy replied, looking right at me. "She could be such a beauty if she would just let down her hair and dress up a bit," he said.

Just as the snake man was turning to see me, I was awakened by the sound of my mother knocking on my door. I gave her a thumb's up sign that I was up. I felt as if I hadn't slept. I was shaking all over and it took me a second to stop. I looked down to see the butterfly and fairy from my dreams were on the back of my hands. What the heck!?!?? I sat there stunned and knew I had to talk to Dr. Wolf.

I dressed and went into the main house to use the bathroom, where I tried to wash the butterfly and fairy off. They bathed in the running water but stayed there no matter what I did. Weird! I ran into the kitchen and got my backpack. I looked up, still confused, and saw Sandy was up and ready for the day.

I felt something rub against my right leg, looked down and heard a loud meow.

"Good Morning, George. Johanna are you ready for school?" asked a voice.

I looked down and saw my cats, Mickey and Garfield. Mickey is a magical black talking cat, a gift from Dr. Wolf for becoming a Secret Keeper. Garfield is an orange tabby with green eyes, old, fat, and can't talk. We found him on our property back in New York. Garfield is kind of a joke in our family. We have no idea how old he is. Every time we take him to the vet, they tell us he is about ten years old. That's been going on for about eight years now. We think Garfield has been taking Botox or something. Maybe he has special powers like Peter Pettigrew from Harry Potter.

My mother came down the stairs, "Ready?" she asked.

We nodded and left for San Juan Hills High School with its huge open campus. It was easy to get good grades.

I said bye to my Mom as she dropped us off, looked at Sandy and said, "I'm off to hang with my friends. See ya later."

"Wait! Did you sleep?" Sandy asked. "You look tired."

As we walked toward my classroom I said, "I had a dream. Well, I don't think it was a dream at all. In fact, I think I was actually at a real place."

"Describe this dream, and I mean all of it," Sandy said.

His demeanor shocked me, so we sat down near my class and I told him. "Um, ok, I'm not super sure where I was, but it seemed like it was a prison on a cliff overlooking an ocean. In the dream, whenever I took a step, the scenery would change. Like I was fast forwarding to where I was supposed to go. It was weird. But I knew I was moving forward. Then the first place where I felt I was able to take a normal step, not leaping, was inside a room., I think it was a cell. There were butterflies of all different colors flying around me. I saw one was injured. But when I reached out to catch it; it turned to blue dust in my hand. Then the scene changed to some kind of laboratory filled with all sorts of medical equipment and stuff. I saw a man about to inject a serum into a little fairy. So, I jumped in between to stop it, and the guy yelled at me to get away. Then the scene changed again to a massive graveyard where there were two men. One was bald, skinny, and had green snakeskin. The other guy was a short with blond hair, and he had weird markings all over his skin. They were talking about testing a serum, and that's it."

I turned away, crossed my legs, and started drawing my dream.

I was really concentrating when I felt hands on my shoulders.

"Aaahhh!!" I screamed

"What are you doing Jo?" asked my friend Sam.

"I'm drawing what I saw in my dream."

"Who's he?" said Sam

"My name's George. Let me see your drawings Rapunzel."

"*Shut up, dude,*" I yelled. My name is not Rapunzel. Rrrrrrrrr.

The bell rang, and we went to our classes. My first class was Bio, then PE, and then to my Resource class. Then on the way to Algebra, I was wishing I could use that fast forward path-step thingy that happened in my dreams. Then I could be to class in an instant! That would be awesome!!

SMACK!! I fell flat on my face and was hurting. Good thing nobody noticed. I guess I don't have magical powers after all.

I fell asleep in Algebra and had another dream about the prison. I had enough control in this dream so I decided I would try and do some reconnaissance work. I needed to figure out what they were using this place for. But my teacher woke me up before I had the chance. Dang it.

The bell rang, and I thought I would try the "path-step" thingy again. My dreams felt so real!! It had to work! I just knew I had magical powers! But this time, instead of ending up flat on my face, I was high in the sky above the school and then falling to the ground! I couldn't breathe! I was panicking! I'm gonna die! I thought. I felt sand against my body pulling me and gently yanking onto the ground. I saw Sandy with a frightened look. Then I noticed I was covered with scrapes and bruises. I was shaking all over. I had a nosebleed, and my glasses were all scraped up too. I got up and walked towards my friends sulking. Sandy tried to help me, but I told him to leave me alone because I was in no mood. I was mad! Why couldn't I made it work?

"Never do that again! You need to talk to Dr. Wolf," Sandy said. "We're to report to him after school for a mission, so you can tell him then."

I rolled my eyes at him. "Whatever." Off to my next class.

It felt like the rest of the day just dragged and dragged. I wanted answers! What was going on in my dreams? Who were the two men? Why were they injecting fairies? And why was there a fairy on my hand and a butterfly on the other one? How could I see them and no one else could?

Finally, the last class was over. As I went through the doorway from my last class, I got dizzy and my head was spinning. I almost passed out when I realized I had just walked through a portal. I thought it would have brought me to the base, but I was on a city street corner instead. Something was wrong. I felt a tap on my shoulder. I spun around with my fist in the air, ready to fight, but it was just Sandy.

"There was a mishap, and I think we are near the base in Spain," he said.

"How come we're in Spain? Why did the portal malfunction?"

"I don't know, but I'm going to call Dr. Wolf and ask."

Sandy whipped out his phone and called Dr. Wolf to see why we were in Spain. I thought we were still in an English-speaking country because the signs were in English.

"All the base portals are malfunctioning. Teams are going to all the wrong places. Headquarters is trying to sort it out," Sandy said and continued, "We're supposed to be in London to receive the mission information from their base leader, not in Madrid. Tommy and Mira were sent to Greenland. Everyone has been ordered not to use the portals and to use other magical means to get to their destinations."

He had a grin on his face I did not like.

Oh crap.

He then grabbed my hand and took off running, right into a wall.

CHAPTER 3

Hellhound

"George O'Gale, are you crazy!?" I
screamed.

Darkness surrounded us. There were
outlines of shapes in different sizes. I saw a light in
the shape of a door. We went through the light and

landed inside a room where Tommy and Mira were getting ready for a mission. They were shocked to see us and gave Sandy a glare of disgust.

"What? How? What were those shapes?" I asked confused.

"That was shadow travel," he replied. "The shapes you were seeing were others using shadow travel. All you do is close your eyes and focus on where it is you want to go. But you must have magical powers for it to work. Too bad for you!" he said with glee. "Stay here while I report in."

Good grief. Learn something new every day my Mom always says. Then an idea hit me. I remembered Sandy said we were going to London, so I thought we could have a little fun and get a head start. Why not give it a whirl? I was able to path-step earlier, well sort of. So, I turned to Tommy and Mira.

"Why don't we play a little trick on our new leader Sandy?"

I stuck out my hands for Tommy and Mira to take hold, and we turned towards the wall where I concentrated super hard on the shadow travel, I had just been through with Sandy. I closed my eyes tightly and repeated the word "London" in my head while focusing on the memories of shadow travel. I held their hands and ran straight into the wall, into the shadows. We were running until we saw the light and stepped through it to the other side.

HA! I did it! It worked!!!! Yippee!!! I knew it! *YES!!!!!!*

We were in an office covered with images and illustrations of all sorts. The room had two chairs, a desk, a glass window, and shelves on two walls.

"May I ask who you three are?" said a British voice. Sitting at the desk was a lady in a blue shirt, average height, pale skinned with blue eyes, and brown hair.

Sandy appeared behind us and said, "We're the team sent by Dr. Wolf. My name is George O'Gale. I'm the team leader."

What? How the heck did he follow us so quickly? Ugh, fail! Darn it.

Well, at least I was able to make it work. I did it! YES!!

"How nice of the doctor to send his son. I'll have to thank him the next time I see him," the woman said. "Son?" What? I thought. "My name is Mrs. Blake. I'm the head counselor for the London base. You're here because we are having a problem with vampires."

"Vampires?" said Tommy and Mira in unison.

"Um, for the record, I would like to state we have only done capture missions and Johanna and I can't do magic," said Tommy

Right? Like wasn't he right there with me as we shadow traveled? Duh?

"Tommy, Rapunzel can do high-level magic. Like me," Sandy informed them.

I snickered.

Wait? What? I thought.

"Back on topic," said Mrs. Blake, "we believe the vampires in London are breeding and hatching dragons. However, it is unclear why, so I'm sending you to see my son to get more information."

We left the building and took a train into the country where Sandy proceeded to get us a cab to a small white house on a cliff where Mrs. Blake's son Isaac was waiting for us. He had dark brown hair, brown eyes, and pale skin. He was standing on the porch.

"What is the mysterious legend and myth of magic?" Isaac asked.

Sandy replied with the Gambit Gang pass phrase. "Magic was considered real in the minds of mortals but is now considered not probable. There are those who know the truth but must keep this a secret." A code of Gambit Gang to make sure it's just us.

> Isaac smiled and said, "Come on in, and I'll
> fill you in."

The place was a mess, so Sandy said, "clean" and the place was crystal cleaned in an instant. Dang! That's cool! I'll have to remember that one. Could come in very handy. Isaac gestured for us to have a seat. "Sorry, I didn't have time to clean up before you arrived. I'm Isaac Blake." Sandy introduced us. "I'm George, and this is Tommy, Mira, and Johanna. Do you mind telling us what's going on?"

Isaac nodded. "We are to retrieve the eggs and dragons the vampires are breeding and gather any further information to figure out what the vampires are up to."

Isaac and Sandy went into the living room while the rest of us moved into the kitchen to have some hot chocolate since we hadn't eaten. We were deep in conversation when I got a deep, creepy feeling throughout my entire body. I started shaking all over.

"Sandy?" I called.

Sandy replied from the other room "Yeah, what is it?"

"Sandy?"

Sandy looked at me and I heard, "Damn. Isaac, take Tommy and Mira now! Go! We'll catch up!" My senses were overloading. That's what happens when something bad was about to happen.

CRASH!!!!

A huge muscular black dog with markings all over, a boxer-like muzzle and razor- sharp claws crashed in from the right side of the house with a man close behind. I screamed and grabbed onto Sandy who was already running. We ran as fast as we could. I could hear the man and dog monster talking as we were running from the house.

"She'll be able to hear us," said the dog. "Quiet Mutt!" I thought I recognized the voice.

"Sandy, that's the guy from my dream. The one who was standing next to the snake man." We kept running.

He must have understood because suddenly, I could hear the dog wallowing in pain.

It was ridiculous how afraid I was. I was still shaking from my overload when I heard Sandy calmly speaking my name. "Johanna, Johanna, Johanna." I stopped and took in a deep breath. Sandy took me in his arms and used shadow travel to get us to a wooded area near the mansion where the vampires lived so we could meet with the others.

"Is she alright?" asked Mira quickly.

"She's all right," Sandy replied. "Just shaken up. Give her a minute. Takes a second for her senses to calm down after an episode."

The weird feeling was dissipating. I could tell I was returning to normal. Sandy let go of me, and I could see everyone was safe. I didn't know if they saw the dog monster thing or not.

"The mission's canceled. We're going back to base, Sandy said.

"We can't end the mission," Isaac objected. "Besides you're not in charge."

Sandy glared at Isaac. "Finish the mission by yourself then, but my team's done."

"My mother won't let you leave until we finish the mission. Trust me; I've tried countless times. She'll only let us go if we complete the mission or if we're all injured or dead."

Sandy looked at his team and asked, "Are you up for it?"

"I'll be fine," I said. "I just need a second."

Tommy and Mira nodded. We had forty-five minutes left before the vampire party started. We all took a breath to calm our nerves. Tommy and Mira sat under a tree, while Sandy and I called Dr. Wolf.

"Hello, Dr. Wolf speaking," he answered.

"Hey, it's me, George. We've got a small problem."

"And by small, he means very big and bad," I muttered.

"What sort of problem?" said Dr. Wolf.

CHAPTER 4

Vampire Party

"Everything started off well," Sandy explained. "We met the team, talked strategy, and then from there things went downhill. Luckily, Johanna sensed a hellhound coming. Isaac got

Tommy and Mira out of there, and I got Jo. She said she recognized him from her dream in the graveyard. When we met up with everyone, we discovered Mrs. Blake wouldn't let anyone leave until we'd finished the mission."

"Tell me about the Blakes," said Dr. Wolf.

"Isaac is half human and half vampire. His mother is human. So, the dad's gotta be a vampire. That much I know."

Silence

Dr. Wolf said, "I'll call you back in a little bit."

Sandy hung up. "This isn't going to end well."

"How come?" I asked sheepishly.

Sandy looked up at the starry sky but never answered.

I left to go horse around with Mira and Tommy. They were playing tag.

"Hey, Mira!" I yelled.

She turned around and started running. I turned around and waited till the last second for Mira to tag me before I used my path step.

"Tag you're it!" Mira yelled.

This time I imagined running down the path to the location. I jumped in the direction and ended in the spot I wanted.

"Not fair!!" said Mira, changing her direction to come after me.
Then I did it again. YES!!! I can do it! We all played for a while until Sandy called us.

Isaac told us the plan. He and I were to act as decoys to keep anyone from going down into the dungeons where the dragons were. Sandy and Mira would get the dragons and the eggs. Tommy could hack into their computer and add a virus to gather information.

Before we left Sandy whispered, "Watch Isaac at all times. Now stand still for a second. "Mist of magic, help me now."

I gave him a funny look wondering what he was thinking. He must have understood the look on my face, so he said, "When you get inside, look in mirror, you'll understand."

We left for the mansion where the vampire party was taking place. Isaac used shadow travel, and I used my path step to arrive in the shadows of the mansion. It was fun using path step even though I did get hurt sometimes. There was a gravel road that led to a giant iron gate. Limos were coming and going. The mansion looked more like a castle. It had four towers with an enclosed courtyard in the middle.

"Who owns this place?" I asked.

Isaac took my hand as we walked towards the front doors. The steps were beautifully carved with mythological images of vampires and werewolves. There were identical twin blond maids about my height, with pale skin, and red eyes, to greet people at the main door.

When they saw us coming up the steps, they spoke in perfect unison. "We've been expecting you. Master Roberts is upstairs waiting for you. Your friend can partake in the party, but she is not allowed to accompany you to the meeting," they said.

I looked at Isaac in confusion, but he never looked back. The inside of the castle was beautiful with crystal chandeliers, with deep dark wood in a herringbone pattern on the floor. There were stained glass windows and beautiful paintings everywhere. I caught a glimpse of myself in a huge mirror on the wall. Nice job. Sandy had dolled me all up for the party. Whewww baby! The guests were dancing as a grand orchestra played music. There were tables set around the dance floor, and I noticed there were people of all ages. It seems there were other creatures attending too.

Isaac let go of my hand. "See what information you can gather here, while I go upstairs and have a chat."

I went to work.

"You should tell your team leader what those servants said," said a voice.

I turned around to see who it was but didn't see anyone.

"I agree with her. I'm Poison Moss. You can call me Moss," said the fairy. The butterfly, "And I'm Crystal. Thanks for saving us."

I looked down at my hands and took off my gloves to see the fairy and butterfly on the back of my hands and realized they were talking to me. I tried to push away my shock and concentrate on the mission. I had a feeling there were probably going to be more surprises. I decided to take their advice and sat at a table. I closed my eyes to concentrate and called Sandy's name in my head.

"What is it, Rapunzel?" Sandy asked.

"The humanoid may be in league with the enemy," replied Crystal.

Sandy instantly yelled, "Who are you?!"

I explained to Sandy who Crystal and Moss were.

"That is an unexpected development. Keep an eye on Isaac," said Sandy.

I put my gloves back on and felt someone tugging at my clothes. I looked down to find a boy, who looked about five years old, wearing a school uniform. I could tell he was a vampire. He had brown hair and one of his eyes was green, the other was blue.

"How come you're not dancing? You've been sitting here for a while," he said.

"That's because I'm not a very good dancer."

"Can I sit with you then? I don't like these parties. I find them boring."

I nodded for him to sit.

"What's your name? Your human but have magic. Can you show me?"

Crystal said, "We can trust the boy. He means no harm."

"I agree," Moss added. "There is nothing to gain from lying to this boy. Go ahead and show him your power."

I felt chills throughout my body and placed my hand on the table. I thought of a mouse and lifted my hand to find a mouse made from snow moving around. Hey, I think I'm starting to get the hang of this?! All right!!

"My name is Johanna," I said, "but you can call me Jo. Now little mouse, go and do my will."

The mouse jumped off the table and went to spy on Isaac.

The boy smiled as the mouse scampered away. "My name is Kevin Roberts. Where did you send the mouse?"

I changed the subject, "Does your Dad own this place?" I recognized his last name from what the twin maids had said. Kevin nodded, still waiting for me to answer his question.

"Can you keep a secret?" I asked.

He nodded, still smiling.

"I'm here to investigate your father and Isaac Blake. That's where I sent my mouse."

Kevin looked surprised and suddenly ran outside to a group of teenagers — five boys and three girls. One of them was a green-eyed vampire. "Tybalt, you need to come with me. A girl is investigating Dad and the Blakes."

I caught up with Kevin, "Why you little liar. Don't you know the meaning of a secret?" Why did Crystal say I could trust him?

"What's going on Kevin?" Tybalt asked. "Is father doing something illegal? So, help me God, if he is, I'll kill him."

I got the feeling I could trust this Tybalt, but before I could talk to him, I started shaking and got an intense headache that almost made me fall over with chills, dizziness, and a head rush … oh no here we go again.

CHAPTER 5

Emergency

I saw myself walking down into a big cave. Dragons peered out at me from behind the bars of locked cells. I could only see their eyes; their bodies were black with no distinct shape. One cell was covered in a thick black cloud. I continued walking and came to a fork in the path where there was a black cloud in front of me covering the wall and a small patch on the floor. Suddenly, the vision ended, and I was back at the party. At least I wasn't shaking. A premonition?

"Your father is accused of breeding dragons," I told Tybalt. "We want to know why and what do the Blakes have to do with it?"

I felt a sudden burst of energy that I used with path step to investigate the vision. What I didn't realize was somehow, Tybalt and Kevin came along with me. Dang it. I'm not quite sure how that happened. I heard them moan in pain.

"Sorry," I said. "I didn't expect you to come with me."

I looked inside a cell and saw it covered in blood, and a picture of a spray-painted monkey with its feet and hands cut off. Someone had written beneath it.

"Touch no evil, Mira."

I looked down at the floor to find severed hands and feet of something; they were unrecognizable. The dragons were roaring like crazy now. I felt extremely sick and was nauscous. White spots clouded my vision, and I was getting dizzy and shaking all over.

"I have to find Tommy. I must. I can feel it."

I felt another burst of energy and used it to path step back to the fork in the path. I was drained and knew I would lose consciousness at any moment. But I held on and used all my strength to get another burst of energy. That's when I saw Kevin and Tybalt passed out on the ground. I looked and saw the spray-painted monkey with his hands covering his gouged-out eyes.

The writing now said, "See no evil, Thomas."

I looked on the ground to find a pair of glasses with eyes. I lost my sight and knew I didn't have much time left before I would pass out too. I cupped my hands together and mustered all the energy and memories of the snow mouse. But I couldn't say the words, so I prayed the two new mice I made would find Sandy to get help. I felt myself hitting a hard surface and knew I was out.

When I woke up, I was in a hospital bed. I was still feeling tired, but glad I had my glasses and could see again. I saw the Egyptian Goddess Bast sitting by my bed reading a book. She had blue eyes and her blonde hair was in a bob. She was wearing a cat-print suit. I've known Bast for a long time as she and Dr. Wolf were remarkably close.

She saw me looking at her, and she said with a sweet voice, "I'm glad you're awake Johanna. You gave us quite a scare."

"Auntie Bast!"

"Seems as though you've had a good recovery."

"What happened after I passed out?" I asked. "What happened to the others? Are they ok?"

Bast smiled but with some sadness. "After you passed out, your snow mice went looking for help. The first snow mouse found George severely injured and unconscious near a computer room. The second snow mouse found the Roberts' friends and brought them to George. George mumbled to call Dr. Wolf, which they did. Dr. Wolf sent a team to bring all of you to the hospital. Tommy, Mira, the

Blakes, and the Roberts' father are all still missing. George is now awake, but they found bacteria eating his magic."

I was worried about my friends, but I knew in the end, everything would turn out alright. Bast left the room and I closed my eyes to concentrate on the third mouse I used to spy on Isaac. I could see the three snow mice.

I said to them, "Go and do my will. Thank you for helping."

I heard a knock on the door and a doctor came in. He had grey hair and bright blue eyes. It was a family friend everyone called Doctor Ricky.

"Hello, Johanna. How are you feeling?" he asked in a jolly voice.

"I'm fine. Can I go home now?"

"You can call your parents, but you can't leave until Monday. On Monday, you can see your parents. This hospital must remain a secret. So, no visitors."

I nodded and said, "Doctor Ricky, can you do me a favor?"

"Yes."

"Tell Dr. Wolf I sent my three snow mice after the Blakes and Roberts' father. Oh, and one more thing, they're creating a serum. The people who took Tommy and Mira."

I had a gut feeling what happened on the mission was somehow connected to my dreams. Doctor Ricky gave me my phone and left. I called my Mom to catch up with her. She was no stranger to having family members in hospitals, especially when it came to being a Secret Keeper and having clumsy triplet brothers. Doctor Ricky had called her to let me know that I was ok. When I hung up, I noticed the date on my phone, and I realized I had been out for three days!!! Bast came back in with some food.

"Holy crap! I was out for three days?" I said.

"You passed out because you were drained of magic. You had used up all of your magic, and if the Roberts hadn't lent you some of their energy, you would not have been able to create those mice."

Bast sat down and said, "Give me your phone." I handed it over. She started dialing.

"Estelle? It's time. You need to tell her everything. It's time for her to know."

Huh??

Chapter 6

Wait. What?

"Mom? What's going on?"

"Oh Johanna, It's no biggy. You're a Magical Autistic," she said with glee

"Wait. What? I don't understand."

"Ok so, I wanted to tell you about the magic, but I couldn't because you were too young, and we didn't know how it was going to work with you. Or if it would even happen. We weren't sure of anything. So, I spoke with Dr. Wolf and he said we should wait. Let nature take its course and see what would happen. But as you were coming into puberty the combination of the magic naturally within you and the Autism you have, created a unique combination. That I always called the A-Card."

"Huh? I'm confused? The A-Card? I've heard you say that before, but what does that have to do with what's happening to me now? Does anyone else in our family have magical abilities?" I asked. My mind was racing trying to figure this out.

"Well no, it turns out your magical abilities were able to come out because you were Autistic. Dad says you have an extra special gene in your DNA. So, when that magical gene is combined with an Autism trait, voila! Dad says the boys may have a magical gene but because they were not Autistic, they don't have any magical abilities. Sometimes when you were little you would sense that something was about to happen. I didn't think anything about it when it was happening but in hind sight it would dawn on me that maybe, just maybe, something else was going on. So, I called it you're A-Card when talking about it with your father. Kind of like code so that we could talk about things infront of you without drawing too much attention to it. We knew that we just had to wait and see what would happen. Dr. Wolf kept indicating that you would have to go through puberty first before we would really know for sure what was going on with you."

I guess that explained things a little. So that's why I can sense something is going to happen? When I'm shaking? The headaches? The dizzy spells, are all symptoms of the combination of the Autism and the magic?

Baffled, I said goodbye and hung up. I was still tired, so I went back to sleep. In my dreams, I visited a forest with rolling hills. There were valleys, tall mountains, lakes of all sizes and meadows covered in beautiful flowers I had never seen before. I walked for a long time and came upon a waterfall, where I could walk right up to the edge. I began to look for fossils, and when I looked up, I saw a wolf sitting there looking at me. The wolf was as white as snow, its claws and teeth were blue. Its eyes were the same color as mine, but it had a sunset purple mark right underneath them. Its mouth was bloody, slimy-looking, and as black as night. The wolf signaled for me to follow. I followed the wolf late into the night. It led me to a huge lake where I followed it into the water. To my surprise, I did not drown when my head went underwater. We kept walking until we came upon a glowing image on the floor of the lake. The wolf laid down and I reached out to touch the outline of the image. I felt an abundance of magic run through my body. I looked down at the glowing image, it was in the shape of a dragon, and the dragon came alive.

CHAPTER 7

Unlikely Game Plan

I heard Sandy's voice calling for me.

"What is it?" I asked in my head.

"How are you doing?"

"I had another strange dream. You'll be glad to hear I sent my snow mice after the Blakes and Roberts' father."

"Tell me about your dream."

"It was about a dragon and other creatures that seek refuge in a mysterious place."

"A dragon?"

"The dragon was the ruler of the forest. A protector that would shelter creatures that were different. To help them survive and do right by the world. Help them when others would not."

"That explains a lot," Sandy said.

I decided to ask him a question that has been on my mind. "Don't you think we are getting along better than usual?"

"Yeah," he said. "It was hard for me to understand what was happening with you. I knew you had some weird quarks and what not, but I didn't understand your Autism. And then who knew you had a special magical gene that allowed your powers to develop to the level they have so quickly. It was confusing. I shouldn't have taken it out at you. I'm sorry, I shouldn't have acted the way I did. I was a jerk"

"What's going to happen when we all get out of this hospital?"

"Headquarters will send a team to try and find Tommy and Mira. I got to go, the doctor's here."

CHAPTER 8
Snow Light

I opened my eyes to find the wolf from my dream lying on top of me with it head on my chest.

"How would you like to hunt down some people?" I asked.

"How many?" she replied.

"Five people. Two vampires, one human, one hellhound and one snake man. What's your name?"

"My name is Artic, so just say the word."

"It's actually a spell."

Cold blizzard.

Silence is your deathly end.

My wolves howl loud.

"Ok," Artic said.

"Bring them back alive, Ok?"

Artic then turned to snow and disappeared. I looked down at the palms of my hands and saw Crystal and Moss. On my right hand there was my ring, a family heirloom. It was a gold band with a diamond in the middle and sapphires on each side of it. When I looked at the diamond, I noticed a small white light inside. I didn't think much of it at the time.

CHAPTER 9

Lockdown & Libraries

I was released from the hospital on Monday. I could have gone home, but instead, I went go to school. I put my hair in a braid and wore a white Rolling Stones t-shirt, blue jeans, and my purple sneakers. I was near my first-period class when Sam came running up to me to give me a big hug.

"How come you missed four days?" she asked.

"I caught a bad virus," I said as we were walking over to Sandy and some other kids.

That was my usual excuse for when I missed school, but they didn't buy it. They think I'm some fighter since when I come back from a mission I'm usually banged up. We talked until the bell rang and went to class. Halfway through class, the alarm rang, and the school went into lockdown. That's weird. The teacher locked the doors and finished the lesson. We worked on homework while we waited for the lockdown to end. But it didn't end until 4:15. I had a strange feeling.

I texted Sandy, "What do you make of this lockdown? I have a feeling that someone's after us."

"Hang on, I'll check it out," he replied.

I texted in the group chat, "Jo, what's happening in UR classrooms?"

They replied nothing was going on, just the boys were using the emergency potty. The lockdown ended, and I went up on the hill next to the school to think. I didn't see anything unusual. My friends were down waiting to be picked up. The police were still lingering around to help prevent traffic issues. I tried to shrug off the strange feeling, but I couldn't shake the thought something might be off. I saw Sandy and went over to sit next to him. He looked extremely tired.

"You look tired."

"I have insomnia, I never sleep, not even a wink."

"Why don't you take some medication?"

"I've tried, even potions, but nothing works."

"That's why you told me to go to bed."

He nodded. I took a deep breath and tried to clear my headache. I always have headaches, but I had learned to live with them since it's part of the Autism.

"Jo are you freezing?" Sandy asked.

"Nope," I shook my head and we headed to my Mom's car since she had just pulled up. Even Mom asked, "Are you cold?" but I said, "No."

"Honey, I can see your breath," she said.

"I think it could be her powers," Sandy explained. We were all still adjusting to my magical powers. Ever since I passed out my magical DNA gene has gone into overdrive. My developing magic was rather unpredictable at this point. So, we all just had to wait and see what would happen next. "Maybe her powers are forcing her body temperature to drop?"

"Yeah? But how far should they drop? Should I be concerned?" I asked.

Sandy shook his head. "Na. The frozen breath is common for people with winter powers. So, maybe you have some strong winter-type powers."

Just then, a call came through on the car's Bluetooth. It was Dr. Wolf.

"Go pick up everyone and head to the LAPD station," he said. "Ask the person at the front desk for the Gambit Gang division. They will take you to the base. I already told your husband and Mickey. I'll explain when you get there."

Dr. Wolf hung up before we could ask any questions. We picked up my brothers, filled them in and drove to LA which took forever with the traffic. And I thought New York City was bad, but then again, they had better public transportation. Sandy didn't speak the whole time. Dr. Wolf and my Dad were there waiting for us.

Dr. Wolf looked worried. "Eric, Estelle, and George, come with me to my office. Kids, Auntie Bast is waiting for you down the hall. Johanna, come back to my office after you say hello to her."

When I opened the door, my cat Mickey jumped onto my shoulders, and Kevin said, "Hi Jo. Can we play?"

"I can't, but I think my brothers will," I said. "Auntie Bast, I'm heading back over to Dr. Wolf's office."

"Alright," she replied. "Now who wants to play a game?"

I left, and Mickey sat on my shoulder and gave me the down low on everything. "Dr. Wolf thinks the lockdown at your school had something to do with the same people who kidnapped Tommy and Mira. We think they are holding the rest of your friends and families." Mickey always had the dirt on what was happening. But this sucked! I had to formulate a plan to get my friends back from whoever was behind this.

I saw my friend Sam sitting in a chair outside of Dr. Wolf's office. Mickey jumped onto her shoulder and whispered into her ear.

Sam looked up at me. "Jo, how come I can see your breath? Are you cold?"

"Later," I said.

Sam nodded as I went inside to meet with Mom, Dad, and Dr. Wolf. Sandy was standing there ready to burst.

"Mickey already explained everything. Can I go?" I asked.

Dr. Wolf nodded. "Go ahead and take Sam with you. She will stay with you until this is over."

I nodded and closed the door behind me. I explained to Sam why I couldn't tell her I was a Secret Keeper before, and about my newly discovered powers.

"Wanna help me with some research?" I asked Sam.

Sam got up and smiled. "Well...I guess that means I'm going to be part of your team!"

I just laughed at her enthusiasm, then left for the Great Library.

The Great Library is a central library hub connected to all the other libraries, colleges, and museums throughout the world. Each library has a person who runs it, and two creatures run the Central Library. I've met one of them and heard bad rumors of the other. The one I met was a good friend of Dr. Wolf, and his name was Mr. Hookthorn. He looks like the dragon that was in

The Goblet of Fire, fighting Harry Potter. Although Mr. Hookthorn was genuinely nice and helpful, unlike the dragon Harry fought. He does have one pet peeve about people asking him why his name is Hookthorn. So, if you ask him, he'll demonstrate by curling his tail and releasing poisonous thorns at you. The other librarian was a giant black and white owl named Swiftsight. He can read your true intentions and if he doesn't like what he sees he won't let you into the library, even though Mr. Hookthorn tries to reason with him. Someone tried to trick him once, and ever since then, Swiftsight has become extremely choosy about who enters. The Great Library was enormous! There were bookcases filled all the way to the ceiling, chairs, tables everywhere, and a front desk with a davit in the wall above where Mr. Hookthorn was curled inside with smoke coming from his nostrils while he was sleeping. There was no sign of Swiftsight, so Mickey lead us to the section we needed. But Swiftsight saw us and flew down to stop us.

"Wait right here," he said, and he flew off.

When he returned, he held a bottle in his claws. "These will help you control your freezing abilities. Use this information wisely."

I stuffed the medication into my pocket. The floor beneath us suddenly lifted and followed Swiftsight to a different library. The flooring disappeared, and Swiftsight flew away as we fell onto a table below us. Sam landed on her butt while Mickey and I managed to land on our feet. A teenage boy came over with black hair, green eyes, and olive skin. He had on a black collared shirt and black jean pants.

He smiled. "Hi! I'm Luke. Can I help you?"

"Yeah," I said. "We need some information on magical travel, snake legends, hellhounds, and vampires."

Sam and Mickey were looking at me in bewilderment.

"What?" I said.

Luke looked at Mickey and said, "Michael? Michael Cast, it's me. Luke Greystone."

Then he turned to me. "By the way, Ma'am, you were speaking in Russian and switched to English."

"Really?! Wow!!" my magic was certainly developing fast! A least I don't have to worry about taking another language in school.

"So, this is where you ended up," said Mickey

Luke nodded and said, "Please take a seat, and I'll bring your books. After the library closes, I will come back to help you."

We took our seats and began to look through the books. Even Mickey was reading, and we were all taking notes. Sam could only read the books in English and occasionally asked for Mickey and me to help. I still hadn't grasped how my magic worked to translate into a different language, so I switched from Russian to English constantly and had to repeat myself.

Several hours had gone by and my mom called. "Johanna where are you guys?" she asked.

"Doing some research and pulling an all-nighter," I replied.

"Check out the books you want and come home. I don't want you out late with all this craziness?"

"Ok, we're on our way."

We gathered our stuff and checked out the books.

Before we left, Luke said, "Jo, tell George I'll write him soon." I was surprised Luke knew my name and George's.

"How do you know our names?" I asked.

"George and I have known each other since we were born," Luke replied. "He often writes about you. We were both adopted by Dr. Wolf, so we're actually brothers."

So, he's the boy in the picture on Dr. Wolf's desk! He had pictures of George, my brothers, and me on his desk since he treated us like family, but there were two people I hadn't recognized in his photos. The other was a girl.

CHAPTER 10

Going Rogue

We pulled an all-nighter, even Kevin helped. The funny thing was, when morning came, I didn't even feel tired. I needed to check in with my snow mice and Artic. I closed my eyes and concentrated on them all. They found the location of the prison and told me the Blakes were assigned to another base. Roberts' father was with the snake man and the marked boy.

I was interrupted by a knock at the door and went to answer it. Luke and Sandy were there, and Sandy looked angry.

"Come on in," I said. "I'll tell you what I found after I wake everyone up."

"Who are those guys?" Kevin asked.

"This is George." I pointed to Sandy and then Luke. "Luke helped us get the books from the Central Library. Kevin, what's your Dad's name?"

"Tim."

I turned to Sandy. "Tim is with the snake man and the marked boy," I explained.

"The Blakes changed their names and infiltrated another base. Artic told me the prison location. She also said Tommy, Mira, snake man, and the rest of my friends were there."

"Good," said Sandy, "then don't go running off to save your friends. Let Dr. Wolf send a team equipped to deal with this situation."

"Does anyone want coffee?" Sam asked.

Luke and Sandy said yes.

"Let me make myself clear. I'll say it again, Johanna," Sandy said, "don't run off and rescue your friends. Let Dr. Wolf send a team. Got it?"

"What makes you say that?" I asked.

Mickey said, "Is that why you wanted me to take you to the library?"

"Yes, Mr. Cast," Luke replied. "We all know the snake is just as powerful as Dr. Wolf and only someone with their level of magical abilities can defeat him. Jo, don't go."

Kevin suddenly realized who we were talking about, "Is this guy Dr. Mez?"

Sam called from the kitchen, "Jo, can you help me for a second?"

I reluctantly got up to help her, but I would have loved to stay and listen to the rest of the conversation. But Sam was persistent. She had a duffle bag across her shoulders.

I mouthed to her, "What are you doing? How did you know?"

"They don't call him Swiftsight for nothing. He left it here with a note" she mouthed back. "He also gave me this letter."

Dear Miss. Chojnicki,

This equipment is waterproof. We gave you a thumb drive with a computer virus, a drive that will send back information, medication with instructions (please read carefully), waterproof glass case, contact lenses, emergency contact information and some clothes for disguises. This plan of yours has morphed into a mission to gather all information on our new enemy and to retrieve as many of your friends as possible. Johanna, you were right not to let someone else rescue your friends. I'm glad you did not trust your counselor until you had all the facts to make a proper judgment. I will send another letter with an explanation of your powers. A few words of advice: don't use any magic because Dr. Mez can sense your magic like I can.

I'm not as bad as everyone thinks.

Swiftsight

I was shocked. I grabbed the duffle bag and Sam. We used the path step to get to the bank of the river by the base. From the library research I did, I had discovered that all types of water were connected through caves weaved beneath the Earth's crust. We took off our glasses and put them into the waterproof cases. The phones and cases went into the duffel bag. We tied a wire around our waists to connect us, so we wouldn't lose each other in the water.

"Are you ready?" I asked.

"As ready as I'll ever be."

"Let's go."

CHAPTER 11

Waterways

We jumped into the water and swam to the cave we needed. We came to a cross current so violent it threw us out of the water. Our wire snapped and knocked us both out. I landed in a tree. I saw Tommy and Mira in a prison cell along with a girl that looked like an angel. They all looked like they were at death's door. I felt sick like when I was in the cell. The angel girl had an aura about her. She saw me, and I realized she had didn't have wings.

She looked a little younger than me. She had short brown hair, blue eyes, freckles, and white clothes.

She said, "We don't have much time, especially Mira. Hurry."

I nodded, and the scene changed. I saw all my friends from school with their families. I got the feeling they were being questioned against their will. Suddenly, the vision changed to Dr. Wolf's office.

"Why did they take Luke and Mickey if they have Johanna and Sam already?" Sandy yelled at Dr. Wolf.

"I guess you guys didn't read Swiftsight's letter," I said, thinking I was still in my vision.

But they looked at me in anger, and Dr. Wolf yelled, "Where have you been!? Where is Sam!?"

It was then I realized I was having one of my weird magic dreams. So, I explained about the letter and how Sam and I planned to get to the prison. I felt intense pain all over my body, but my head hurt the worst. Sandy left and came back with the letter. They read it and were still angry.

"How did you plan to get there?" Sandy asked.

"We jumped into the river and swam to the current that we needed. Then we suddenly came across a violent cross current, we were thrown up and out of the water. The wire snapped, and we were knocked out. I ended up in a tree and started having visions, which is what brought my out of body experience to you."

"Describe your visions," said Dr. Wolf.

I did, just before waking up with searing pain, I found myself upside down in a tree. I began to yell for Sam. To see if she was okay and to get help to get me down. I tried not to move as I didn't know how high I was off the ground. I thought I heard someone call my name, but the pain was getting worse. Then I was freefalling and then a loud hard slam against the ground. It took me a moment to get my bearings. The world was turned right side up again. There was a canyon full of tall trees with a river. I saw Sam standing over me. She was a bit roughed up with scrapes and bruises, but somehow, she'd gotten me out of the tree.

Sam said, "You're welcome."

"Thanks."

I sat up and retrieved the second letter Swiftsight had given us out of my bag.

Dear Miss. Chojnicki,
    Your Magical Autism has given your abilities that are exceptionally rare. You're an ice witch. You can use the power of ice for medical use. So, you can freeze a wound, and the ice will melt healing the wound. You can freeze your body to the absolute point you won't get wounds at all. But there is one drawback, you will appear to stop aging. Sam can hold and use other people's magic, but she can't create magic of her own. For this mission, you should give your power to Sam so Dr. Mez won't discover you.

There is a lot more than you'll need to know, but you'll discover magic on your own, and you will receive further training during the summer.
Swiftsight

I looked at Sam and asked, "Did you read the letter?"

Sam nodded. "Yeah, I did, and I have to say, you guys are weird. But I'm willing to do anything if I get to do stuff like this again."

I smiled and stood up to see the white wolf Artic sitting on the bank of the river. I had sent her on a mission to help us track our friends and luckily using her keen senses, she had found them. We used shadow travel to get us to where our friends were being held. When we arrived at the prison from my dreams, we all changed into the disguises Swiftsight has provided. Sam was a secretary, and I was a nurse. I heard some moaning, and I turned around to find Sandy soaking wet and mad, from exiting the water of the beach.

"What the heck are you doing here?" I asked.

"Seriously?" Sandy wore a strange look. "Dr. Wolf sent me to keep you under control. He's had enough of you going rogue."

Sam gave him a towel.

"You're not bringing us back, are you?" Sam asked.

"Let's just get this mission done and over with," he said with a tone.

"How did you find us?" I asked.

"Swiftsight told me. I beat it out of him. Now let's go."

CHAPTER 12

The Mission Begins

The prison was exactly how I envisioned it in my dreams but with people. It looked just like any other prison. The name on the building said Manus Prison. We checked in at the front desk and Artic showed us the way. We had her disguised as a therapy dog. Sam stayed by the lady who checked us in. She was nice and told us where Sandy and I needed to go. I hugged Sam and transferred all my powers over to her through a big hug. Then I split off from Sandy, who didn't tell me who he was supposed to be impersonating. I wore scrubs and a

"Joan" nametag and Artic went with Sam to help her. I used my fake ID to walk into the prison's hospital. As soon as I walked through the door, I got knocked down and held against the wall. Someone had their arm across my body restraining me. Their left hand pulled my head back by my hair revealing my neck. I felt something dripping down my neck. I was lifted off my feet as a voice said: "Let me leave, and I won't kill the girl."

I heard a growl in his voice, and I tried to get a look what it was. I saw tiger fur. Sirens were wailing now. The room was covered in red lights flashing, and there were footsteps.

CHAPTER 13

Tiger Strike

"Let her go, Greyson. I know you don't want to be experimented on again," someone yelled.

Greyson growled.

"Don't be so nice to him. Don't give him a chance." I heard another voice yell.

Then there were two loud shots right near my head, and I fell to the ground with a thud. I got away from Grayson, and I saw he was out. He was like Dr. Wolf but a tiger, and he had a more human face than that of an animal. I turned around to find three security people and nurses bringing a straitjacket, muzzle, and stretcher. To my surprise, Sandy was one of the security officers. The other one was black skinned, grey eyes and as tall as Sandy. The other security officer was muscular, short hair, tan skin, blue eyes. I noticed something was off about the two security officers, but I didn't think much of it.

"Joan you're bleeding," Sandy said. "You should get cleaned up."

The black security officer looked at Sandy's eyes and said, "Jonathan, I'll take her."

He introduced himself as Prometheus Titan and his friend as Geronimo Mez.

I asked, "Is he related to Dr. Mez?"

Prometheus looked at me with a suspicion and said, "Not by blood."

I then looked more closely at his arms and found a tattoo of the creative hammer on his arms. Creative hammer tattoos are only found on giants. Prometheus must be a giant, but how can he be regular sized?

CHAPTER 14

Memories

He brought me to the medical room where a young nurse girl was waiting. She was beautiful, about my height and had black hair with bangs, olive skin and blue-green eyes with deep black eyeliner.

"Come have a seat," she said. "My name is Zoe Nightshade."

Prometheus closed the curtains and stayed. I sat on the bed and Zoe put her hands in a bucket of water to cleanse them. Then she took out her hands and placed them on my neck, healing my wounds.

She looked at Prometheus and said, "We can trust her and her friends."

She then placed her hands back into the bucket and repeated the process until there were no signs of injury.

I closed my eyes and heard Crystal say, "Focus on your powers and then open your eyes."

I did what she said, and to my surprise, I could feel I had a new magic ability. I thought I had transferred all my powers to Sam, but apparently, I was able to create this new one. When I opened my eyes, I looked at Zoe, and I could see her life story and her true thoughts and intentions. It was something indescribable. I then turned my gaze to Prometheus, and the same thing happened. I tried expanding my gaze over the entire hospital wings just wishfully wondering how far my gaze could go. It worked! I could see everyone was under a mind-controlling spell. Only Sandy, Zoe, Prometheus, and a couple of the patients were not. I knew Zoe and Prometheus wanted to save everyone, but they were afraid of Dr. Mez's ramifications. I could see the truth of the situation all around me. I could see Zoe, Prometheus, and Geronimo had been taken from their families by Dr. Mez, and he wanted to wage war against the Gambit Gang! But I couldn't see why.

CHAPTER 15

Snake Encounter

I got off the bed.

"Get me a computer," I said. I knew I could help Zoe and Prometheus.

The ground started to shake violently. We were knocked to the floor. The shaking stopped, and we got up. It had stopped just as suddenly as it started.

"What was that?" I asked.

"Dr. Mez must be beating Grayson and Sinbad to make them obey."

"What?!"

The curtains drew back, and Dr. Mez came in. He looked like he did in my dream

"Are you Joan?" he asked.

I nodded my head yes.

"You will deliver medications to the patients," he commanded, "and you will document your observations on their charts."

I nodded that I understood.

Dr. Mez continued, "Ms. Nightshade will show you the schedule."

Dr. Mez left, and Zoe helped show me around the hospital and where we were going to be staying. The hospital seemed normal except the patient rooms were cells suited to the specific experiment being performed on that patient. I was staying in an administration looking like building, but on the inside, there were bedrooms with bathrooms on the upper levels while general gathering areas occupied the first floor.

I started thinking about Zoe being experimented on, so I asked her during lunch, "Were you guys experimented on as well?"

Zoe replied with her mouth still full of salad with another question, "Us experimented on?"

I nodded my head. "Yeah, like altered?"

Zoe sat there thinking for a while before she answered. "I was supposed to be a simple healer, but now I'm a water spirit. Prometheus was a craftsman in the spirit realm, now he is a warrior. Geronimo was supposed to be a normal wolf, but now he has the ability of fire with hellhound powers. There's others too."

There was a lot I didn't understand, I knew I would just have to wait until I got to magic school to figure out the details. I assumed I would go during summer break. After lunch, Zoe showed me my medical rounds. I gave her the computer virus and told her how important it was to upload it. Sam would have installed another virus in another section of the facility by now. So, we were covered.

CHAPTER 16

New Game Plan

My room was big enough for a bed and a wardrobe. I was on the same floor as Zoe, and we were neighbors. I unpacked and got ready for bed. I decided to chat with Sam telepathically for a little bit before passing out for the night.

"So," I asked, "how's it going?"

"Ok. Everyone seemed normal, but I met two girls who I knew had been experimented on by Dr. Mez. They asked for my help."

I thought Zoe and Prometheus were the only ones not under Dr. Mez's spell?

"Hang on a second. I'm going to try to do a mental group chat, so we can go over everything together. Everyone, you need to gather your memories, to join the chat.

Everyone popped up, even the people Sam was talking to.

However, Sandy was still singing a song when he popped in. *"Oh Angel, do you remember the times I called you angelfish? That is when the family wanted me to give a man cement shoes and make him go swimming in the city river."*

Dr. Wolf was the one who finally interrupted Sandy's song. "I remember singing that song to you."

"Crap!" Sandy cursed when he realized he was singing in front of people. I mustered my strength to expand my power to check and see what the true intentions of the girls Sam was talking about might be. I could see they were identical twin, redheads with black eyes and peach-colored skin. I started the introductions.

I said, "I'm Joan."

Sam went next. "My name is Cherry Sunshine, and I love cupcakes."

"Seriously?" said Sandy. "I'm Johnathan Moon."

Then Dr. Wolf. "My name is Dr. Jambar Wolf, and I am here to stop Dr. Mez."

Zoe and Prometheus introduced themselves and explained they had been experimented on by Dr. Mez. The twins introduced themselves as Mea and Mia Heartlock and told us they had been experimented on too.

"Please tell me everything you know about Dr. Mez, his experiments, and anything else you know."

They each went on to explain their own story and what had happened to them.

"They were spirits that had taken on human forms. Grayson has strength and invisibility powers. Sinbad is stronger than Grayson and has a long scar on his right eye," said Zoe.

Dr. Wolf said, "Thank you Ms. Nightshade. And you two girls?"

Mea explained their powers. "We are called China Dolls because we can transform into movable dolls. We also have a yin-yang power."

Sam asked, "What's a yin-yang power?"

Sandy explained this one, "Because identical twins are born from a single cell
and soul they can switch powers with each other as long as they remain in opposite positions like water and fire."

Mia then spoke, "Two girls, Sirena and Silk, are loyal to Dr. Mez. We don't know what powers they have."

Sam piped in saying, "Oh and there's someone else we should be concerned about. His name is Mark Twist."

Dr. Wolf said, "I've heard of him. But I'm more concerned about Dr. Mez. So, let's focus on defeating him first. We're going to have to fight them. Nightshade and Sunshine will stay behind to help Doctor Ricky retrieve the prisoners."

A teenage boy appeared saying with a gleeful growl, "We will join you to get our revenge."

He had spiky-black hair, a long scar that started in his hair went through his right eye and down to his chin. Grayson appeared next to the newcomer, but he appeared more human except for his eyes which were cat like and blue. Grayson had short, flat and black hair and his nails were made of metal with sharp ends.

"And who are you guys?" I said with concern.

Zoe pipped in, "That's Sinbad."

Dr. Wolf growled and asked, "Can we trust them?"

I replied, "Yeah, they're honest."

"Speaking of trust and truth. Why don't you tell us your real names since we told you ours?" said Sindbad. "Enough with the charades."

Sandy answered before Dr. Wolf could do anything. "I'm George O'Gale. And I'm here to get my brother Luke Greystone back."

"You're from Dr. Mez's first batch of experiments. They called you the Moon Experiments, and your brother the Ghost Experiment," said Prometheus.

Dr. Wolf banged his cane. Oh boy. A spell was cast, and instructions appeared in our minds.

"Silence! No one else will disclose their true identity and no one will know what each person's job is. The spell will end once the mission completed. You all need to learn to trust one another."

After that Dr. Wolf vanished and left us alone.

The China Dolls said, "Hold up the number of the batch you were a part of."

The China dolls held up four. Grayson and Zoe held up three. Prometheus two, Sandy and Sinbad held up one finger and Sam, and I made a zero sign to signal we had not been experimented on. We all looked at Sandy and Sinbad because they didn't fit the pattern of a year apart and yet were one of the first to be experimented on.

Sinbad explained, "To be honest, I was summoned from the soul world to assist in an experiment. But yes, my biostructure was examined. I am like Dr. Wolf but when I came here, I didn't know that."

I felt sad for Sinbad because he was taken from his home. I was getting very tired, so I gave everyone a warning that my telepathy was going to end soon.

"Guys I'm getting tired, so this will end soon."

Sinbad said, "Go to bed I'll take it from here."

CHAPTER 17

The Speeder, The Whiner, & The Angle

Before I completely checked out for the night, I quickly took a mental check on my friends being held captive by Dr. Mez. I needed to make sure they could hang in there until we could rescue them. I could see they had some wounds from being kidnapped and I still had enough energy to use my healing magic so they wouldn't be suffering. Tommy, Mira, and the angel girl instantly healed.

Mira asked quickly, "Johanna what is going on? Where are we? Who is she? Are you ok? Is everyone in the group, ok? Is Tommy ok?"

I knew she had just to let it all out, and I waited until she finished.

She continued, "I was doing a final check to see if we got all of the dragons. When I felt a pinch on my ankle, and I passed out. I only just woke up."

I piped in quickly, "Hold on, Mira, let me hear everyone's story first and then I'll explain everything."

"Same as Mira," said Tommy.

Looking at the angel I said with sympathy, "I know you're an angel and they took your wings so why don't you tell me your story."

"My name is Elizabeth, but feel free to call me Lizzy, and I'm thirteen. I came to the mortal world on my own to investigate a demon. When I came across a snake that bit me on the leg. I then woke up in this cell with these guys unconscious and realized my wings were gone," she said.

I noticed a beautiful wind chime sound when she spoke, and I said, "Tommy we are working on a rescue mission. We'll get you to a hospital ASAP! Be patient a little longer, we're working on it."

CHAPTER 18

Battle Preparations

I immediately opened my eyes and started packing my bag. So much for getting some sleep. I slung my bag over my shoulder and went to wake up Zoe. She was sleeping when I arrived, so I shook her. Dr. Wolf planned that Zoe and I would go on ahead of everyone to set up a barrier spell.

I asked Zoe, "Do you mind if I change here?"

"Not at all."

We got changed into our black combat clothes and went through the portal. We were in the

Grand Canyon, and it was sunset. It was deserted, which was good so no innocent bystanders would get hurt.

"Question? How are we going to see in the dark and how do you make a barrier?"

I heard a buzzing noise behind us, and we turned around to find Dr. Wolf on all fours covered in armor. His armor had war carvings all over them: his teeth, nails, and tail were also covered in metal, and his eyes were blue gems.

Dr. Wolf said, "Armor, now become a part of me."

The armor disappeared, and his coat glistened with a glow, and swirled in the wind.

"Whoa!" we both said in unison.

Repeat after me, "Ember of flames, of fire, let me see what you see. Starlight, Star sight."

We repeated what Dr. Wolf said, and suddenly we could see in the dark.

We both said, "Whoa," again.

"Draw a large circle with you in the center. Then write the names of the people we are fighting in the circle and write the words 'cancellation barrier' in the center. When you've drawn the circle say out loud "expand" five times."

"Zoe, when you're finished, go back to the hospital and let Grayson and Sinbad out of their cells."

I asked, "How are we supposed to do this?"

Dr. Wolf laughed and said, "Use your ice to make a pen with ink for us"

I did what he asked, and my ice pens turned out to be a bit thin and long, and the ink was white. We drew the circles and made the circles expand. Zoe left to do as she was told.

CHAPTER 19

Here we go!!!

I saw a zillion spiders coming towards us.

"This is it!" Dr. Wolf cried. "Fight with everything you've got!"

I held my palms up facing the spiders to freeze them, and I thought the barrier would work. So why are they still coming?

Dr. Wolf leaped to my side and said, "Activate barrier."

But the spiders kept coming. Dr. Wolf's fur was standing on end. He swished his tail and released needles killing the spiders. I just kept trying to freeze them.

"Why isn't the barrier working?" I asked.

"I don't know. The spiders shouldn't be able to step foot inside the barrier."

I went into the center of the three circles and wrote the words. "Ice cancellation barrier." I did the same in the area where they were linked together. The barrier began to glow, and ice began to form. It was working! The spiders began to retreat.

"Nice thinking! But this fight isn't over yet," said Dr. Wolf.

I nodded and tried to look for people mentally. I could hear harps and spun around to see where it was coming from.

"I can't see anyone."

Dr. Wolf said with a groan of anger, "I can't believe I was so foolish as to think creating this kind of barrier would work. They must be out of range of your sight."

We were waiting for them to strike when I recognized the music. It was from an animated movie I had seen.

"Have you seen the animated version of the movie 'Hellboy'?" I asked.

"No," said Dr. Wolf looking at me quizzically.

"In the movie, there was a spirit that played a Japanese harp to controlled spiders who were her children. I think she used her spider silk, to make a web, and the web was vibrating to create the music and causing the spiders to go where she wanted them to go."

"Perfect deduction, young lady, but your greatest test has yet to come," said a silky voice.

A gold light beamed behind us. George, Sinbad, and Grayson suddenly appeared ready to fight. Sinbad had two swords squared off at the end. One was half the size of the other blade. Grayson's had a tiger on it. George pulled two small voodoo-looking like dolls out of his pocket.

The silky voice began to speak, "I see reinforcements have arrived and with some traitors, but it will not help you when the good Doctor arrives."

Sinbad made a growling noise.

Dr. Wolf asked Sinbad, "Do you recognize the voice?"

"You should recognize the voice too. That's Charlotte," said Sinbad critically.

Charlotte began to speak in a creepy silky voice, "My, my, how you've grown Sinbad."

Sinbad stuck his short blade into the ice. I placed my hands on the floor and imagined an ice barrier. I used my thoughts to make thick layers of ice to reinforce the barrier. I heard a high-pitched scream and then saw a green flash. Sinbad stuck his long blade through the ice in Charlotte's direction. She was wearing a dress in the pattern of a spider's web made from her silk. It was beautiful but eerie at the same time. She rose onto her eight long legs screaming and spewing green fire at us. Sinbad used his powerful magic to absorb the barrier into his sword. The energy was transferred up through the short blade, through his body, out the other side through the long blade and towards Charlotte. She dodged the attack and screamed again, spewing more green fire. Sinbad stuck his blade again in Charlotte's direction. She again dodged it. Suddenly there was a buzzing sound from Charlotte's direction. A cell phone text came from Dr. Mez. Charlotte answered it with one of her legs and then quickly stomped another leg with a bang and said, "Location shift."

The scene changed, and we were in a large clearing surrounded by a jungle. The barrier was completely gone, and we were unprotected. When I looked to my left, I saw green liquid coming at us from Dr. Mez, and Charlotte was spewing green fire. Sandy created a sand shield just in the nick of time. The green liquid hissed as it dissolved in the sand. I noticed a few droplets had gotten on me, so I froze the spots to heal myself. I heard my friends moan in pain and I quickly healed them by putting a thin layer of ice throughout their bodies. Sandy threw up another sand barrier to protect us.

I quickly closed my eyes while the barrier was up and took a mental check-in. I could see Luke had gotten through the barrier, but he didn't look like he was on our side anymore. There was a black piece of something floating in the air. It looked like a black shard of glass. I grabbed it with my right hand, and it suddenly it burst into bright white flames that exploded in the air. I yanked my arm away, and Luke collapsed. My right arm was completely scorched, but I felt no pain. I could see my breath. I quickly froze my hand with ice to heal it. Luke was lying face down. Sandy ran to Luke's side and flipped him over revealing his front covered in blood. He looked dead, but he moaned when Sandy flipped him over. I used my ice to heal his wounds. All while the green liquid and the fire kept burning through the barrier.

Sandy asked me, "Why did you attack Luke? Is he going to be all right?"

Crystal said, "Yes, he'll be fine. She healed him with her ice powers. But who knew you were a balancer?"

I asked out loud, "What's a balancer?"

Dr. Wolf answered, "Luke will be fine, George. Johanna just freed Luke from Dr. Mez's hypnotism. She eliminated the memories of Dr. Mez ever having cast a spell on him. Balancers are people that can change memories or eliminate the memories all together. We'll talk later. Sandy's barrier won't hold her off for long."

Sinbad said quickly, "We should split into teams."

Sandy threw the two voodoo dolls that were now covered in blood, into the air and said, "Reconfiguration original form."

The voodoo dolls turned into the China Dolls.

Sinbad said, "Pair up and fight!"

I had a feeling Dr, Mez was as powerful as
Dr. Wolf, and I was nowhere in their league with
my magic. The barrier suddenly dissolved. They
attacked all at once. Dr. Mez with the green liquid
from his mouth while Charlotte was throwing green
fire. Geronimo and Mark also attacked with fire,
while Sirena used with a high-pitched voice. I
instantly created an ice barrier by placing my hands
on the ground. Once the barrier was up, it shattered
from the force of the attack. Sinbad and Dr. Wolf
unleashed an attack of their own to try and buy us
time to escape.

Sinbad said, "Implement the ideas."

Sinbad's plan went into effect. Everyone
broke off into teams to battle. Sandy turned into
glowing gold sand in humanoid form. I saw the
China Dolls, and Mark Twist moving to the right of
the clearing. Mark Twist had turned into a
hellhound, and I knew he was the same hellhound
Sandy had beat up earlier. Grayson put Luke on his
shoulders and took off to the left of the battle with

Geronimo after them. I used my path step to keep up with Sandy, the Sirens were coming after us. Sirena was wearing a white dress, and her hair was short and curly.

I said to her, "You know a dress is bad for combat."

In turn, she said a spell, "Ghoul wail," that sounded like a scream and it was powerful enough to disorient me. Sandy was affected too. It made him revert into a human. He was stumbling around when I got to him. I grabbed him and took a massive leap with my path step. After several more enormous leaps, we had put enough distance between us, but we could still hear the wail. We began to run on foot, but we were feeling nauseous. I wasn't looking where I was going when I stepped on a bomb with my right foot. Sandy was still running, not realizing what had happened. My magic had gone. Sandy stumbled back to me.

"My magic is gone; I can't freeze the bomb."

Sandy buried us in the sand just before I heard a loud explosion.

My right leg was hurting. When the sand cleared, we had been blown to a different area close to where the China Dolls were fighting. I could feel my magic slowly returning. The pain went away, and my whole leg was covered in one big bruise. Finally, the wailing spell wore off, and so did the nausea. Our heads were clearing, and we could see Sirena, but she couldn't see us yet. I quickly shot an icicle into Serena's mouth to freeze it shut before she could let out another wail. Sandy grabbed Sirena with his sand and said, "Paralyze."

The sand disappeared, and Sirena fell to the ground. I ran to her and grabbed the black glass which was on her right shoulder. The black glass burst into flames and then shattered. I pulled my right hand away, and again my hand was all scratched up.

CHAPTER 20
Next Move

Sandy looked at me and said, "We should find Bomb Voyage, and force him to deactivate any bombs."

"What? What about Sirena? We can't just leave her here and who's Bomb Voyage?"

"We'll come back for her later, but right now Bomb Voyage is our top priority, he's the one who made the bomb that could steal your magic away. Dr. Mez likes to have Bomb Voyage around so he can collect the people who get trapped. All he has to do is wait for his next victim to come and step on a bomb then he collects his prize."

"Why don't we just detonate the bombs instead? Then we can free anyone who's trapped!"

"Because if we can take out Bomb Voyage then we will be putting a major dent in Dr. Mez plan, and he won't be able to collect any victims to run experiments on."

Oh.

"If looks could kill, you'd be a serial killer. Now let's go."

He started walking, "Oh, Mr. Sandman."

He turned and smiled. "First please help me with Sirena and then I'll help you find the bombs."

"Help me carry Sirena," I insisted.

Sandy picked up Sirena with this sand, and I directed him to a tree big enough for Sirena. I placed my hand on the tree, and with my other hand, I pulled Sirena in and gently placed her inside. The tree would make a nice hiding spot.

Sandy said, "Nice thinking."

"Now let's get Bomb Voyage."

Sandy started walking behind me when I pointed out, "Hey, follow in my steps or you might step on one of Bomb Voyage's bombs."

Just then we heard an explosion a few yards ahead.

I said, "That's in the direction of the China Dolls."

"Let's go," he replied.

CHAPTER 21

The Bomber

We ran as fast as we could to the China Dolls. When we arrived Mark Twist was down for the count, and the China Dolls were fighting some man. He was a scrawny little guy with brown-slicked hair, and he wasn't carrying any bombs. When I looked at the China Dolls again, I realized they weren't attacking; they were defending themselves. Bombs circles were at their feet the same kind I had stepped on.

"Welcome to the party. I hope you enjoyed your first victory because this time you'll lose," said Bomb Voyage.

A bomb circle began to appear, and we jumped. Sandy landed in between the China Dolls. I took the opportunity to use my path step to get behind Bomb Voyage and gave him a powerful kick that sent him flying into a tree. Sandy engulfed himself and the China Dolls in sand to get out of the bomb's range. Luckily the blast was small since I had put up a shield to stop most of it. However, I accidentally kicked Bomb Voyage into the blast. But Bomb Voyage detonated another bomb at the same moment that canceled out the blast. He still hit a tree headfirst which left him unconscious. I hid him away inside the tree.

"Well that was unexpected," said Mea.

"You can let go of us now, Mr. O'Gale," said Mia.

George let them go, and I asked, "What do we do now?"

"We need to help Grayson," said George.

The China Dolls objected. "Grayson can handle Geronimo, he's strong enough. We should go help, Dr. Wolf and Sinbad."

"Dr. Mez and Mrs. Charlotte are stronger than all of them put together," said Mia.

"Don't underestimate Dr. Wolf," said Sandy.

Then we heard a howl from Dr. Wolf's direction.

"If you can hear me, then come back from where we came," said Dr. Wolf.

"See, Dr. Wolf defeated them," said Sandy with a smirk.

"Let's get going," I said.

"Oh, Johanna, aren't you forgetting about the prisoners?"

I completely forgot about Sirena and Bomb Voyage. The worst part was I forgot which tree I had hid Sirena in.

"Oh, um, by any chance do you remember where we hid Sirena?" I asked with a smile.

"Since you're the one that hid her, you can go get her," said Sandy.

Sandy covered himself, the China Dolls, Bomb Voyage and Mark Twist in the glowing gold sand and disappeared.

CHAPTER 22

The Other Side

"Really!?"

I started concentrating on Sirena's magic, so I could find her. I began to walk around and quickly found her. I used path step to get us back to the others. Everyone was there except for Geronimo, Dr. Mez, and Ms. Charlotte. The others were beaten up, and bleeding but still standing.

"Hello Jo. I see you have survived your first real battle. I see you have freed the young lady as well, which reminds me. Thank you for healing me," said Luke with a smile.

I smiled back and said, "I'm glad that—"

I was suddenly heaved into the air, turned upside down and thrown headfirst into the ground with the image of horror on my friend's faces. I was out cold. I was under the frozen lake where I had met the dragon. There were strange skies above and dragons. Snow was falling. It felt like the Arctic but peaceful.

"How are you feeling Johanna?" said a familiar voice.

"Uh, I'm fine, thank you. Who are you?"

"I'm Ember, the Queen of this realm. I am the dragon you've seen carved on the bottom of the lake."

"Why is everything under water? Why are you in this form? Why does this place seem so like my grandfather's place? Can I go home?" I was tired.

"Johanna, my past life before I came to this realm forced me to use most of my power to give peace and create this sanctuary. Unfortunately, there are people scared of my powers, and they have sealed me away under this lake. The only way I can help people is by giving my powers to someone else. I trust you, Johanna. I'm asking you, if you can use my power and do good in this world. Your answer will be shown through your actions. You are free to leave whenever you want. But beware, if you ever do evil in this world, you will lose not only my power but everyone you know in this realm as well."

I got up and thought for a moment about the huge amount of responsibility I was being asked to take on. I knew in my heart this was my calling.

I needed to get back to my friends, they needed me. I thought about returning to their world and realized something was missing in the lake. I closed my eyes and concentrated on the lake. The fire was the element that was missing. To ignite the flames, I first thought of my memories of being angry. But I knew that would make the flames burn the water. Then it came to me; the flames will fill me with pride and love. I gathered all the memories of my family and friends and turned them into flames that lit up the lakebed. I swam to the surface. Moving through the water was hard like in my dream. As I approached the surface of the ice, I focused my magic on my right hand to punch through the ice. But the ice didn't break. I thought to use the fire, which melted the ice and I climbed through the opening. I stood there breathing in the fresh crisp air.

I heard a voice calling, "Miss we haven't got all the time in the world to dilly dally. Now come on the train. We have a schedule to keep."

I looked around to find a train that reminded me of the one in the Polar Express movie. The conductor had a blue uniform, brown hair, brown eyes, and white skin.

He was holding a lamp in his left hand and cupped his mouth with his right yelling, "Come on now Miss! We have to get you home!"

I ran to him just a few yards away.

The conductor helped me in, "When this door glows, open it and step through."

He closed the door before I could say anything. I sat down on the left bench and looked out the window. The train began to move at top speed. The sky was strange, everything was frozen, and this world was beautiful. The door began to glow when the train stopped at a town called Hollow Eve Light. The door glowed, I opened the door and stepped through.

CHAPTER 23

Hospital

When I opened my eyes, I had four boys on top of my hospital bed asleep. Three of them were my brothers and the fourth was Kevin Roberts. His brother Tybalt Roberts was reading a book in a chair.

"Why am I piled under boys?" I asked.

Tybalt looked at me and said, "Good you're awake. Let me go tell your mother and the doctor." He got up and left.

"But you didn't answer my question," I said.

My Mom, Tybalt, Bast, and Doctor Ricky came in.

"How are you feeling, Johanna?" Mom asked.

"I'm fine Mom, just tired, and a bit confused."

"All right boys, the doctor needs to examine her now," said Bast.

Mom and Bast got the boys off me.

"No magic, missions or gym class for the rest of the school year. You'll have to do physical therapy till summer. You have a concussion, a bad knee and you're also knock-kneed by the way. Which won't help, but I will leave you this. You'll be glad to hear you succeeded in saving all your friends, plus Mr. Greystone, Sirena, Dr. Mez's test subjects and all the prisoners. Job well done Johanna!"

With that, he left.

Then my Mom scolded me for making her worry.

"Johanna, I am so happy you are safe. But I'm angry. You didn't get permission from Dr. Wolf. You made us think you were kidnapped. And we thought you were dead! You're grounded. You're to do all the chores in the house when you get home. Only then can you go on a mission and you WILL follow the rules. If you mess up even once, you'll never go back as a Secret Keeper, is that understood missy?!"

"Sounds fair for the crimes I have committed."

Tybalt studied me, and Bast said, "That's a good girl. Now, boys time for you all to go home."

The boys and Bast said goodbye, gave hugs, and left. I told my Mom about the mission, the strange dreams and how much fun I had.

Tybalt remained quiet whenever my Mom was in the room, but when my Mom left for a few minutes, he said, "Allow me to introduce myself formally. I'm Tybalt Roberts, and I'm glad to see you are recovering well."

We shook hands, and he continued. "Our brothers have become friends, and I hope we can too."

"Are vampires normally this formal or is it just you?"

He smiled "It's proper to be polite, but all vampires do have an objective behind every action."

I asked, "And what's your objective with becoming friends with me then?"

BOOM!!!!

"What was that?"

Tybalt got up and opened the window and looked around and a lady on the loudspeaker said, "Code Red. I repeat Code Red. Sedation is required. Code Red."

Tybalt sat down and said, "Payback. Sinbad keeps running amuck and pulling pranks. Don't worry about it, it's nothing. I, on the other hand, want to help the Gambit Gang. Act as a mediator, so you won't start a war."

"Who's Sinbad?"

"Sinbad…"

Mom entered the room, and Tybalt picked up his book and continued reading. My Mom sat down and began to read. Dang it.

"Excuse me, I'm sorry but visiting hours are over. You have to leave now," said Zoe from the doorway.

Doctor Ricky must have offered Zoe a job.

"Glad to see you're awake Johanna. We'll catch up later," she said.

Everyone left, and soon dinner was served. It looked terrible, so I didn't eat anything. I was totally bored so I went back to sleep. I heard a knock and Sandy was at the door.

"Come in."

He read my chart and came over to the left side of my bed.

"Scooch over. We need to talk. "Regular clothes," said Sandy.

My clothes changed to the regular clothes I normally wore. I scooched over, and Sandy laid down next to me with his right arm underneath him.

"Can you give me an update on everyone? And yes, I'm already grounded."

"It was Geronimo who did the attack, it should have killed you. After that, Dr. Ricky took control of the hospital. All the people working there vanished. All your friends wanted to become Gambit Gang, so Dr. Wolf let them. Dr. Wolf lost his ability to appear in human form, and Sinbad gained another talented eye. Prometheus found his grandmother and now is living in Louisiana. Grayson and Zoe started working here at the hospital. The China Dolls met a lady named Madame Mountain and are studying under her. Geronimo got away. Luke is back in the library and me, well, I want you to stop being a Secret Keeper and tell me where Queen Embers' Realm is."

I looked at him in complete confusion but noticed his eyes were red and not blue.

I felt afraid, and I asked nervously, "Why do you want me to stop being a Secret Keeper? Why are you asking about Queen Ember? Why are your eyes red?"

"Where should I begin, well, how about convincing you that you're awful at being a Secret Keeper. Every time you made a friend, they became a Secret Keeper. But then you got all your friends captured, hypnotized, and drugged. You almost got yourself killed, twice. You're a terrible fighter, and you don't have natural killer instincts. And you are the most annoying person I know, and you have a power that I need."

He got up went to the right side of my bed and shot me with a red medical pen. I got intense waves of numbness, and he just laughed. I got up from my bed and punched him in the jaw. Then, punched him in the chest, stomach, and shoulder.

He was still laughing and said, "There is one thing that I love about you, and that's your stubbornness. Too bad George won't let me take you with us. I'm Sahara, Mr. Sandman's other half, the demon of dreams. Goodnight little princess. Have wonderful nightmares."

My vision was going, but I wasn't about to give up without a fight. I went at him with punches, flips, and magical attacks. But the drug was working fast! Sahara punched me in the neck with sand and I was down for the count. When I woke up, I was on my own.

The Gambit Gang

Epilogue

In January, Johanna got ready for her birthday weekend, while Bast and Dr. Wolf were talking in the kitchen. They were whispering. Elizabeth, Sinbad, and the Roberts were in the living room waiting for Johanna to come downstairs.

Bast said, "Sweetheart, you need to tell her everything. She deserves to know, she's old enough know."

"I know, I know, I'm just still in shock. Sahara never tried anything like this since the incident with Lula. Now he tried something with

Johanna. I'm worried we may never get George back."

"You don't need to worry about that, you do need to worry about having the conversation with Jo."

"What do you mean I don't have to worry about George! I'm his father, of course, I'm worried about him."

Bast had a grin on her face.

"What are you planning?"

"Don't worry… I'll give you until Johanna goes to summer school to talk to her, but if you haven't by then, I will tell her myself. Sooner or later she will find out everything, whether it's from you or me. You sent Michael after George, right?"

"Yes."

They heard Johanna's footsteps and stopped the conversation. She came downstairs with her bag packed. Bast had decided to take Johanna to Las Vegas to see a Cirque de la Soleil show for her birthday.

"Alright everyone it's time to go," Bast said.

They said their goodbyes to Dr. Wolf, who could not attend since he had lost the ability to appear as a human after his fight with Dr. Mez.

He hugged Johanna goodbye, and mumbled under his breath, "I'm sorry Lula."

"Who's Lula?"

"It's nothing. I didn't realize that I said anything," said Dr. Wolf.

Johanna thought that could be the name of the girl in the photo on Dr. Wolf's desk. She thought about it the whole ride to Vegas. She opened some of her presents in the car, but two presents had no names from their senders. One was a bracelet with a pyramid charm, and the other was a marble-sized crystal ball.

After seeing a fabulous show, Johanna thought the night was over. Elizabeth heard a knock on their hotel door. She opened it to find Sinbad and Tybalt holding a finger to their mouths to signaling her to be quiet. Elizabeth nodded yes and held the door open. Sinbad and Tybalt rolled Johanna up in her bed sheets and carried her out of the room. Elizabeth got her glasses, phone, and dress clothes and followed them. They gently placed her on the floor.

"Surprise!" they yelled in a loud whisper.

"What's going on?"

"We're going to a party! My Mom's throwing it," Sinbad said. Sinbad was Bast's son. They had been separated when she came to this dimension.

"That's so awesome!"

"Here I'll help you change into these clothes," said Elizabeth.

The girls went into the bathroom to get ready. Kevin said, "I can't believe that worked!"

"I can't believe that little angel believes us," said Tybalt.

"Of course, they would, my Mom throws the coolest parties ever, so why wouldn't they believe they're going to one of my Mom's parties?" Sinbad said.

When the girls came out, all three of them said, "Wow. Nerd got an upgrade."

She came out in a black outfit with long black gloves that looked stunning on her. They used shadow travel to get to the party, but this was no ordinary party. The party was a Ghoul Bash filled with magical creatures. Johanna quickly sensed the boys had been tricked into coming here. They decided to play along and have some fun singing and dancing the night away. A little while later, Johanna got lost trying to find the ladies room, when she overheard someone saying George's name. She pulled out her phone to video the conversation. There were two boys, one with red hair and a white mask that covered his eyes, wearing a suit, and he had a sword on him. The other boy had a dark royal-blue hair. She stopped recording because she thought they were done talking but they had started talking again. She tried to video again but accidentally took a photo with a flash. Johanna freaked out and took off running to find Elizabeth. While she was running, she telepathically reached out to her friends.

Tybalt said, "Sinbad already headed home. My brother and I will meet you at the hotel."

"I got Lizzy," Johanna said. Lizzy was Elizabeth's nickname.

Johanna meet up with Elizabeth and shadow traveled back to their hotel room, where Bast was still sleeping. Elizabeth and Johanna went to the boys' room to see if they made it back okay.

"Is everyone back, Tybalt?"

"Yes, now go back and get some sleep. We keep this between ourselves, for now, agreed?"

"Agreed," Johanna and Elizabeth both said at once.

Everyone went back to bed. During breakfast, everyone notice Sinbad was missing. Bast was furious that Sinbad had snuck out. Tybalt shot the girls a look to keep their mouths shut. Luckily

Sinbad showed up hours later and took the blame for everyone. They headed home and never said a word about the party.

To be continued?

The Gambit Gang

Look forward to these titles coming soon…

The Gambit Gang
Summer School

Paranmormal Investigation Unit

The Last Resort Agency
L R A

The Gambit Gang